Annie's Anger

(CBT worksheets)

A CBT THERAPEUTIC METAPHOR BOOK
FOR CBT CHILD THERAPISTS IN TRAINING

Dr Nicola Ridgeway & Dr James Manning
Illustrated by Irena Urosevic

Annie wasn't the sort of girl who wasted time on how she looked. She was the sort of girl who pulled her red curls up into a scruffy bunch and threw on ripped shorts and a t-shirt as they were the best for having fun in. After all, there were so many exciting things to do when you were ten: climbing trees, riding a bike. There was simply no time for mirrors.

Annie lived on a tree-lined street with her Ma, Pa and little brother, Kenny. Luckily, Annie's house was just a five minute walk from the park, which was also her favourite place in the world.

There were so many things to do there: she could see her pals, play on the swings and, best of all, pat people's pets. Annie often met Mrs Holland and her dog, Scrappy. Scrappy was always trying to lick Annie's face, even though he knew he wasn't supposed to. Annie never grew bored of the park.

But today, was not like other days.

Annie didn't understand what was happening to her, but she was overwhelmed with so many feelings.

'Annie, it's time to get ready to go out,' said Ma, walking into Annie's room. Ma always set time aside to get ready. Today her shiny, red curls were combed perfectly, and she'd pinned a flower to her dress.

'Its a lovely day to go to the park,' said Ma cheerfully.

'The sun's shining. It's so unlike you to still be in your room.'

'I don't feel like going out today,' whispered Annie.

'Why ever not?' asked Ma, looking concerned.

'I don't know!' squeaked Annie. 'I just don't!'

'How about a nice bowl of cereal?' suggested Ma trying to cheer her up. 'I've got the cereal with raisins in, the one that you love.'

'I'm not hungry,' grunted Annie, throwing herself onto her bed and pushing her face into her pillow. 'Just go away, Ma.'

Her mother looked at her for a second. 'I'll be back in a minute.'

Ma did not intend to give up on her daughter so easily. After checking on Kenny and getting his breakfast ready, she went back upstairs and knocked on Annie's bedroom door.

Annie was still lying face down on the bed with her face pushed into her pillow.

'Come on, Love,' said Ma, stroking Annie's hair. 'We really have to get ready to go out. We need to drop Kenny off at his friend's house.'

After Ma left the room, Annie struggled to get herself dressed. But, finally, she did it. Then, she forced herself to go down to the kitchen.

‘What’s wrong with you?’ shouted Annie’s younger brother Kenny as Annie ambled into the room. Kenny looked a lot like his sister, just smaller, with identical red curls. And, just like his sister, his laces always seemed to be undone.

‘What’s it got to do with you?’ Annie answered snootily. She was in no mood to talk to her little brother.

‘I know what it is.’ Kenny smiled impishly. ‘You’ve got hormones,’ he whispered, covering his mouth so that only Annie could hear. ‘I heard Pa say it to Ma and he said that he had a nightmare about you getting bigger and turning into an angry monster. Ha! Ha!’ he chuckled.

Kenny then started to sing the most annoying song imaginable. His song was so whiny and high-pitched that Annie covered her ears to make the noise go away. Ma even left the room, saying that she needed to fetch something from her bedroom. Kenny then stopped singing and started to chant under his breath, 'You've got a boyfriend. You've got a boyfriend. You've got a boyfriend. You've got a...'

'No, I haven't,' shouted Annie interrupting her brother. 'Be quiet!'

But Kenny didn't listen and kept on going.

This was the final straw for Annie. Suddenly, she snatched up Kenny's bowl of cereal and tipped it over his head. Kenny was so shocked, he didn't know what to say. So he just sat there in silence.

At that very moment, Ma returned to the kitchen. She looked at Kenny in horror. By then, most of the milk had meandered all the way down Kenny's body and was dripping onto the vinyl floor. Drip! Drip! Drip!

'Annie!' bellowed Ma, looking shocked. 'Go to your room this second!'

'What happened Kenny?' Ma asked her son, as she helped him up to his bedroom to change his sodden t-shirt.

'I don't know,' whined Kenny. 'She just picked up my bowl of cereal and threw it all over me.'

'I'm sure there must have been more to it than that,' said Ma, eyeing him suspiciously. 'Your singing was even driving me crazy. Did you say anything else to her to make her angry?'

'Nothing' squealed Kenny. 'I promise.'

Up in her room, Annie sat on her bed. She had never done anything like this before, and she didn't know what to expect from Ma. But she knew Ma would want to talk about it. Sure enough, there was soon a knock on her bedroom door.

'Can I come in?' asked Ma softly.

‘Okay,’ answered Annie. She felt her shoulder’s relax; Ma didn’t sound angry at all.

Her mother sat on the bed next to her.

‘Annie, you haven’t been yourself lately. What’s wrong? It’s not like you to behave in this way.’

‘He was winding me up,’ grumbled Annie. ‘It was his fault. He made me do it!’

‘There is no way that Kenny could make you pick up the bowl and pour cereal over his head. I think what just happened has been bubbling up for a little while, and it just boiled over like a saucepan left on a stove.’

Annie didn't say anything and just stared at her hands.

'You know you can talk to me about anything, don't you?' said Ma. 'I know you've been very upset about something because the other day I saw that

your computer had a big crack in the screen. I don't think that it happened by accident. Is this how you have been dealing with your feelings?' asked Ma.

'It's the only way to make me feel better,' sobbed Annie, looking frightened and embarrassed as she shoved her head into her pillow. 'You don't know what it's been like for me.'

'How about you tell me what's been happening at school lately,' said Ma.

'It's too complicated,' sighed Annie.

'Just start at the beginning,' suggested Ma gently, 'and we'll see what happens.'

Annie felt tears welling up in her eyes as she began explaining things to her mother. She struggled to get her words out and started to cry. 'You know my best friend, Jenny? Well, we were playing basketball, and our team was losing. Jenny wouldn't pass the ball to me because she wanted to score all the baskets by herself, and I know she was doing it on purpose because Jordon was watching.'

‘Who’s Jordon?’ Asked Ma.

‘He’s just a boy at school,’ said Annie with a dismissive shrug.

Her mother frowned. ‘Just a boy?’

‘Okay, he’s a boy that Jenny likes.’

‘And how about you?’ asked Ma knowingly.

Annie let out a sigh. ‘Okay, I guess I like him too. We both like him.’

'And?'

'And,' Annie ballooned her cheeks, 'all she wanted to do was to score so she could impress him, so she wouldn't pass the ball to me. Jenny scored a basket and was running around bragging.'

'What's the problem with that? Wasn't that good for your team?'

'I got so frustrated that I pushed her, and she fell over. I promise I didn't push her that hard. I think she fell over deliberately. The teacher saw it happen and sent me off. It was so embarrassing.

I had to watch the game on my own from the side. And, to make things worse, our team lost. Everybody blamed me, and no one wanted to sit with me at lunch.'

'What happened with you and Jenny afterwards?' asked Ma. 'She's been your best friend for years.'

'We got into a bit of a fight,' mumbled Annie.

'A bit of a fight!'

'She pushed me, and I accidentally hit her in the eye. Mrs Jones noticed a mark on Jenny's face and asked us what happened.'

'So, did you tell her?' asked Ma.

'Neither of us would say,' said Annie smugly. 'So, Mrs Jones sent us both to the headteacher.'

'Oh, oh - Annie!' spluttered Ma.

'We had to sit outside Mr Harris' office whilst everyone walked past us. Everyone was laughing and sniggering. It was so embarrassing. I wanted to disappear.'

'What did Mr Harris say?' asked Ma looking a little concerned.

'He told us that he would be sending a letter to you and to Jenny's mum. Then he kept going on and on about the school's ethos and respect; stuff like that. You know how boring he is. He sends everybody in his class to sleep.'

'Then what happened?'

'He made Jenny and I go around the school picking up litter. It was terrible and humiliating. A lot of kids were dropping stuff on the floor just to see if we would pick it up.'

'So, what happened between you and Jenny after that?' asked Ma.

'We haven't talked yet,' replied Annie.

'You're so similar and you often like the same things. It's no surprise that you both liked the same boy,' said Ma. 'You were both so full of feelings that it was difficult to think properly. It must have been tough for you. Both of you were trying to impress this boy. But, in the end, you were both left feeling embarrassed because you felt that you had made fools of yourselves. Does Jordon know about your fight?'

Annie shrugged. 'I don't know. I'm not interested in him anymore. I think he's spending time with this girl called Lucy now. I just feel awful about hitting Jenny. I didn't mean it.'

'I know you didn't mean it,' said Ma as she stroked Annie's back.

Annie let out a long sigh.

‘I think I understand what’s been making you feel the way you have. You felt bad about hurting Jenny because you care about her. You felt a little jealous about Jenny being noticed by Jordon. You felt frustrated because Jenny wouldn’t pass to you. You felt sad because you thought that you had let yourself down, and you felt frightened about being in trouble with the teachers. You were dealing with a lot of feelings at once,’ said Ma.

Annie let out another sigh.

'I guess I have,' replied Annie. 'I didn't know you could have so many feelings all at once.'

'Would you like to be friends again with Jenny?' asked Ma.

'Yes, I would,' said Annie nodding.

'Okay, Love,' Ma nodded and patted her daughter's hand, 'I'll do my best to help you with that. I'll have a chat with Jenny's mum today.'

'Thank you, Ma,' said Annie. 'I don't know why, but I feel a little better now that we've had our chat.' She stood up. 'I think I'd better go and say sorry to Kenny.'

'You do know why Kenny teases you. It's because he adores you and wants you to see him,' said Ma.

'Yes, I know,' said Annie as she started to walk out of the door. Annie turned and looked back at her room. For a reason that she could not fully understand, her room seemed a much happier place than before.

The following week Kenny stole Annie's teddy bear and 'performed' surgery on it, removing the teddy's eye so that he could turn it into a pirate.

It was Annie's favourite bear and she was very upset. However, after talking to Ma about her feelings, she forgave Kenny.

After Kenny completed his punishment - dish washing and vacuuming - Ma walked with Annie and Kenny to the park. For the first time in a very long while, Annie allowed her feelings to just melt away...

The End

Printed in Great Britain
by Amazon

33644340R00020